The Dog Who Sang at the Opera

written by

Jim West and **Marshall Izen**

illustrated by

Erika Oller

Harry N. Abrams, Inc., Publishers

*To all the supers at the Met,
two-legged and four-legged, and the millions
of children we have performed for
—J. W. and M. J.*

*To Edite, with thanks
—E. O.*

$\mathcal{P}$asha was a beautiful dog, and she knew it. Whenever Pasha and her owner, Shirley, went for a walk, people turned to look. *My beauty makes me a queen!* Pasha thought, and stuck her pointed nose high in the air.

Shirley worked at the Metropolitan Opera House in New York City, playing the piano and helping the singers learn their music. Operas are plays in which everyone sings instead of talking.

One day she came home very excited. "Pasha, I have wonderful news. We're doing an opera called *Manon,* and we need a beautiful dog onstage during the big festival scene. You are going to appear at one of the greatest opera houses in the world!"

Yes, yes, thought Pasha coolly, *of course.*

The next day Shirley took Pasha to the Metropolitan Opera House—
the Met—for a rehearsal. There were dozens of people on the big
stage. There was another dog, too.

What a scruffy thing that is. What could he be doing here? wondered Pasha,
looking down her long Russian nose. *Oh, no! He's coming this way!*

"Hi!" panted the little dog. "My name's Sluggo. What's yours?"

"My name is Pasha—*Miss* Pasha to you," she replied, turning her head away.

"Have you ever been in an opera before, Miss Pasha?"

"No," snapped Pasha. "But I listen. On the radio."

"Oh, they're great! We've been in three of them. My master, Sam, is a clown, and we do tricks together."

"A clown dog?" sniffed Pasha. "And what *breed* of dog are you?"

"I'm a mix," Sluggo answered cheerfully.

"You're a mutt," barked Pasha. "I was bred by royalty in Europe. *Je suis une reine.* But you wouldn't understand French. It means I'm a queen!" She held her head high.

"But it's fun being related to lots of different kinds of dogs," answered Sluggo. "Oh, look over there. That's the director."

"The director?" asked Pasha

"He's very important. He tells us all what to do." There was a tug on Sluggo's leash. "Oops, the director's gonna talk now. We've got to go. Bye!"

The director made a speech and told the singers and other performers where to stand.

When he saw Pasha, he smiled and patted her head.

"You are so well behaved and beautiful, you must stand next to our diva, Manon."

"The diva is the biggest star in the opera!" Shirley whispered to her. "Good girl, Pasha!"

Pasha looked at Sluggo smugly. "I told you I was a queen," she said.

In the costume room, a lady put a sparkling necklace on Pasha and gave Shirley a long, fancy dress.

Pasha noticed that Sluggo was given a particularly silly-looking pointed hat and a ruffle to wear around his neck.

The next morning was the dress rehearsal—practicing the opera like a real performance. Everyone loved the big festival scene. As the singers sang, acrobats flipped and twirled behind them, tightrope walkers teetered overhead, and puppets performed on their own small stage.

Sam the clown came on in a brightly colored costume with Sluggo right beside him. Sluggo wore his pointed hat and walked on his back legs! Pasha was horrified. Sluggo even jumped through a hoop!

Next, Manon sang her big song, which is called an aria: "The Gavotte." Her voice was the most beautiful sound Pasha had ever heard. But that didn't matter. It seemed to Pasha that all eyes were on her—the glamorous wolfhound in the dazzling necklace.

That night Pasha had a wonderful
dream. She was on the stage of
the Met, in a red dress, singing.
She was a diva! Everyone was
applauding and cheering,
"*Brava*, Pasha! *Brava!*"

Shirley gave a little tug at her leash. The conductor looked up. Pasha heard some of the people in the audience giggling and thought excitedly, *It's just like my dream!*

She sang even louder. "Wa-hoo, woo-*hooo*... *Wa*-hoo-woo-*hooo*-woo," she sang, giving it everything she had. "Woo-*hooo*. *Wa*-hoo-woo-woo-*hoo*-wooooo."

The louder she sang, the louder the audience giggled. *They love me!* thought Pasha. She loved being a diva! Her voice blended with Manon's voice and the glorious sound of the Met orchestra. There was applause, but Shirley quickly pulled Pasha off the stage before she could even take a bow.

All the stagehands were laughing. Shirley was giggling, too, but she was upset with Pasha. She knelt beside her, looked into her eyes, and said, "Pasha, Pasha, dogs are not supposed to sing in the opera. Never, ever!"

The director was not laughing. He told Shirley that Pasha could not be in the opera anymore.

No sparkling necklace. The costume lady took it back.

While Shirley took off her own costume, Pasha sat down
in a dark corner. She had never been in trouble before.
She was beautiful. She was perfect. This wasn't
supposed to happen.

"Are you all right, Miss Pasha?"

Pasha closed her eyes and turned away. "This is
not a happy time for me. Please, I want to be alone."

Sluggo looked at her, huddled in the corner.

"I thought you sang beautifully, Miss Pasha."

"No, no, please, go…" Pasha opened one eye. "You really think so?"

"Honest, Miss Pasha, I thought your high notes were better than Manon's."

"*Spasibo*," whispered Pasha with a slight smile.

"What's that mean, Miss Pasha?"

"It's Russian for 'thank you.'"

"You're welcome," answered Sluggo. "That's English for 'any time.'"

The next day there was an article in the newspaper about Pasha, the dog who sang at the Met. "You're famous, darling!" said Shirley, laughing. The phone did not stop ringing all day.

That weekend, all of Shirley's friends, including Sam and Sluggo, were invited to her apartment for a concert. With Shirley at the piano, Pasha sang Mozart. Then she sang to music by the Russian composer Tchaikovsky, and everyone applauded politely.

But when she sang "The Gavotte" from *Manon*—her big number—they all stood and cheered, "*Brava,* Pasha! *Brava!*"

Sluggo waited until all the people had finished fussing over her. Then he came over. "You look beautiful tonight, Miss Pasha."

Pasha beamed. *"Spasibo,"* she murmured.

"And you sang better than ever," said Sluggo. "I heard Shirley tell Sam that the Paris Opera might be interested in you, Miss Pasha."

"Oh, Sluggo. You don't have to call me Miss Pasha. I was being silly. Please call me Pasha."

Sluggo's eyes shone. "I hear we're going for a walk together—Pasha. Tomorrow."

Now Pasha, Sluggo, Sam, and Shirley go for walks together almost every day. But on Saturday afternoons, Pasha curls up in front of the radio and listens to the live broadcasts from the stage of the Metropolitan Opera House. She pretends she is there once more, wearing her jeweled necklace, standing beside the star.

And as she listens, she remembers what a beautiful voice
Manon had . . . for a human.

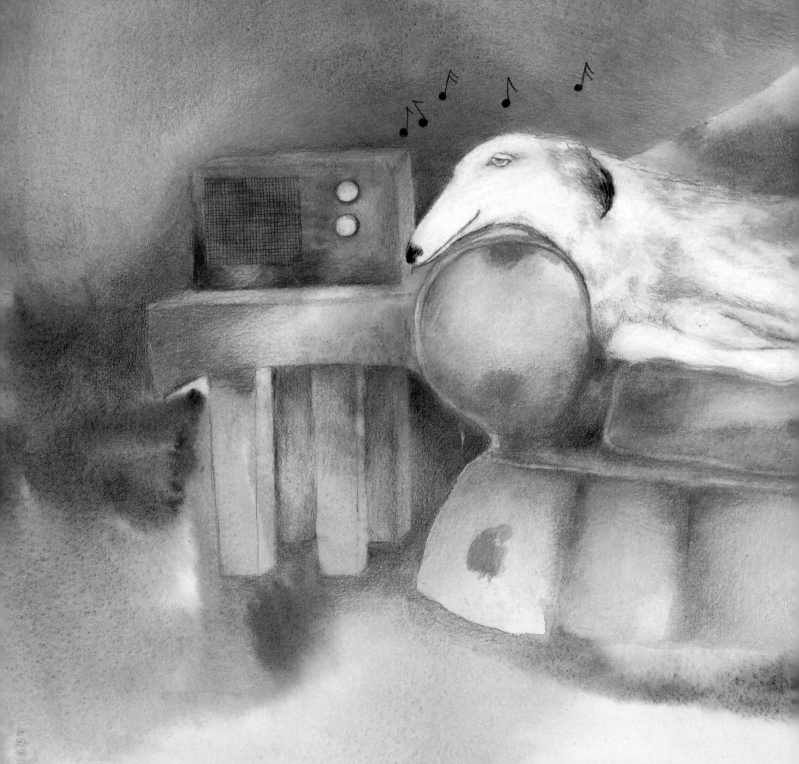

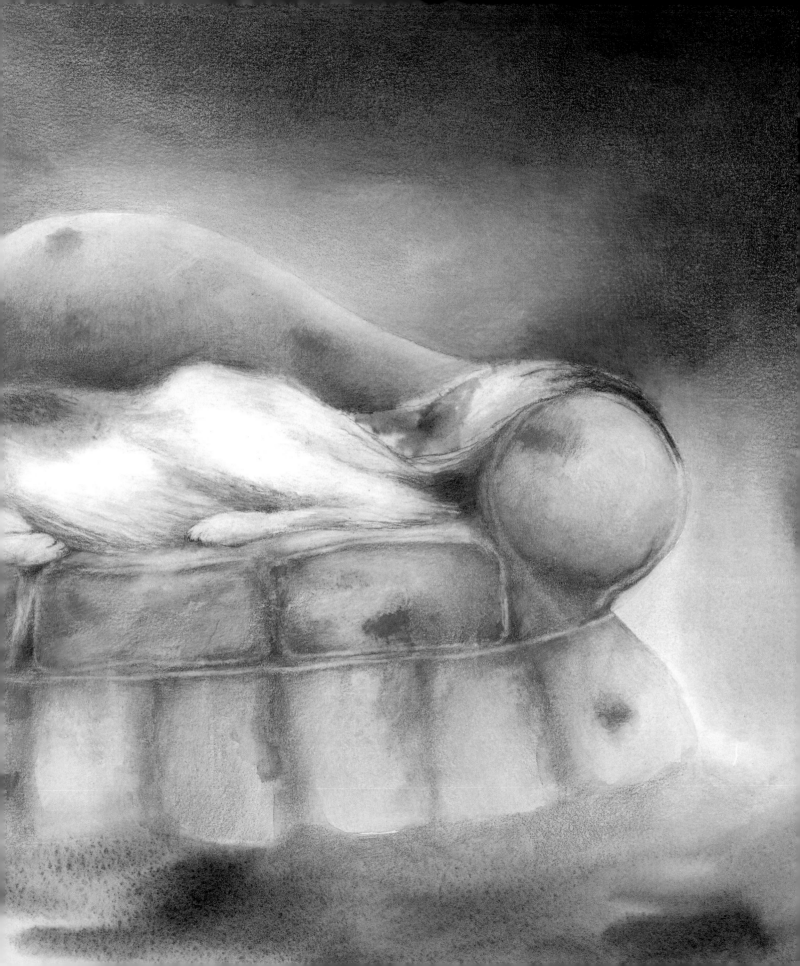

This story was inspired by a true event that took place at the Metropolitan Opera House in New York City on September 26, 1997. The authors, Jim West and Marshall Izen, were onstage as puppeteers when a dog named Pasha, or Passion, really did begin to sing along with the star, Renée Fleming.

Pasha

Renée Fleming

Chronicle

■ A Russian wolfhound competes with a soprano

A soprano's best friend? In the case of **RENÉE FLEMING**, it's not Pasha, the Russian wolfhound who was to have appeared on stage during this season's Metropolitan Opera production of Massenet's "Manon."

On Friday, Ms. Fleming, in the title role, was singing her most demanding and dramatic aria when, she said yesterday, "I heard an uncanny sound, as if someone was singing along with me backstage."

"The audience started to titter and I couldn't imagine what it was," she continued.

It was Pasha, a canine supernumerary, part of a crowd scene in the second act.

"After the first part of the aria, the handler who was on stage holding the dog for a tableau walked the dog off," Ms. Fleming said. "I told the director, 'It's the dog or me.'"

For tomorrow evening's perform-ance, there will be no dog. Meanwhile, Ms. Fleming is trying to figure out what it all means.

"I haven't decided yet if this was the most humiliating experience of my career or the greatest compliment," she said.

A newspaper article about the event.

RENÉE FLEMING

October 17, 1997

Dear Ms. Latham,

Many thanks for your kind letter. And please pass on my thanks
to your dog, too, for giving herself, me, and the opera in general
the best publicity we all have had this year! The story made it into
The New York Times, *USA Today* and the *International Herald
Tribune*. It seems it went around the country as well, as I know the
story also ran in my hometown of Rochester, NY. Now we know
what makes the news in an opera house.

I am a dog lover and my family owned three English Setters at one
time, so I certainly do understand how unpredictable animals can
be. My comment about "the dog or me" was completely tongue in
cheek, however I confess I am relieved not to have the competi-
tion anymore. I thought Passion's high notes were at least as
good—or perhaps even better—than mine.

I hope and trust you both enjoy many more years of performing,
and send fondest best wishes to you both,

Renée Fleming

Renée Fleming

A letter from Renée Fleming to Pasha's owner, Susan Latham.

With special thanks to Susan Latham and Passion.

This book is not authorized, sponsored, or endorsed by the Metropolitan Opera.

Design: Angela Carlino
Production Manager: Jonathan Lopes

Library of Congress Cataloging-in-Publication Data
Izen, Marshall.
The dog who sang at the opera / written by Marshall Izen and Jim West ; illustrated by Erika Oller.
p. cm.
Summary: Pasha, a dog who believes herself to be beautiful and perfect, joins the company of Manon at
New York's Metropolitan Opera House, but on opening night she cannot resist singing along with the diva.
ISBN 0-8109-4928-8 (alk. paper)
[1. Dogs—Fiction. 2. Opera—Fiction. 3. Metropolitan Opera (New York, N.Y.)—Fiction. 4. New York
(N.Y.)—Fiction.] I. West, Jim, 1954– II. Oller, Erika, ill. III. Title.

PZ7.I96Dl 2004
[E]—dc22
2003025792

Text copyright © 2004 Jim West and Marshall Izen
Illustrations copyright © 2004 Erika Oller

Printed and bound in China
10 9 8 7 6 5 4 3 2

Harry N. Abrams, Inc.
100 Fifth Avenue
New York, NY 10011
www.abramsbooks.com

Abrams is a subsidiary of